The Billy Goat in the Chili Patch

A Mexican Folktale
Adapted by

KEO FELKER LAZARUS

Illustrated by CAROL ROGERS

STECK-VAUGHN COMPANY
An Intext *Publisher*
Austin, Texas

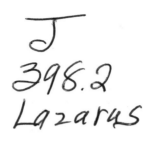

Adapted from a translation
of "The Ram in the Chili Patch"
from *Folk Tales of Mexico*.
Translated and edited by Américo Paredes.
Copyright © 1970 by
the University of Chicago Press.

Library of Congress Cataloging in Publication Data
Lazarus, Keo Felker.
  The billy goat in the chili patch.
  SUMMARY: When a number of animals fail to get the
billy goat out of Pepito's chili patch, Pepito calls
on a lowly ant.
  [1. Folklore—Mexico]   I. Rogers, Carol, illus.
II. Title. III. El Borreguito.
PZ8.1.L353Bi3   [E]   75-39636
ISBN 0-8114-7743-6

ISBN 0-8114-7743-6
Library of Congress Catalog Card Number 75-39636
Copyright © 1972 by Steck-Vaughn Company, Austin, Texas
All Rights Reserved
Printed and Bound in the United States of America

Pepito lives in Mexico. He takes care
of his mother's chili patch.

Every morning Pepito carries water up the hill
for the chili plants. Every evening he hoes
the ground to keep the weeds away.

Pepito is proud of the chili patch.

Mamacita is proud of Pepito.

One morning when he reached the chili patch,
Pepito found a billy goat eating the green
chili leaves. "Billy goat! Billy goat!
Get out of the chili patch!" Pepito cried.

But the billy goat only took another mouthful
of leaves.

Pepito ran and waved his arms in the air. "Go away! Go away!" he yelled.

The billy goat glared at Pepito. "Go away yourself, you unmannerly boy! This is my chili patch now!" And lowering his head, the billy goat ran at Pepito and tossed him out of the chili patch.

Pepito scrambled to his feet and clapped his
hands to the sides of his face. "The billy
goat will eat up Mamacita's chili patch!"
he said to himself. "What shall I do?"

A gray burro came plodding up the hill.

Pepito ran to him. "Good-day, Señor Burro,"
he said. "You are a strong animal. Please,
will you chase that billy goat out of the chili
patch for me?"

The burro flopped his big ears. "Why certainly,"
he said, trotting up to the billy goat. "Billy goat!
Billy goat! Get out of the chili patch!" he brayed.

But the billy goat only waggled both ears and took
another mouthful of green leaves.

The burro turned around and kicked at the billy goat with his sharp hooves. "Go away, billy goat! Go away!" he snorted.

The billy goat glared at the burro. "Go away yourself, you stupid burro! This is my chili patch now!" And lowering his head, the billy goat ran at the burro and tossed him out of the chili patch.

The gray burro stood up and shook himself to the end of his tail. "I am sorry I cannot help you," he said to Pepito.

"Thank you for trying, Señor Burro," Pepito said.

A spotted dog came trotting by.

Pepito ran to the dog. "Good-day, Señor Dog," he said. "You are a cunning animal. Please, will you chase that billy goat out of the chili patch for me?"

The dog wagged his tail and ran at the billy goat. "Billy goat! Billy goat! Get out of the chili patch!" he barked.

But the billy goat only waggled one ear and took another mouthful of green leaves.

The spotted dog crept forward and snapped at
the billy goat's heels with his sharp teeth.
"Go away! Go away!" he snarled.

The billy goat glared at the spotted dog.
"Go away yourself, you cowardly cur! This is
my chili patch now!" And lowering his head,
the billy goat ran at the dog and tossed him out
of the chili patch.

The dog picked himself up and shook the dust out of his fur. "I am sorry I cannot help you," he said to Pepito.

"Thank you for trying, Señor Dog," Pepito said.

A fighting cock came pecking along the road.

Pepito ran to the cock. "Good-day, Señor Cock," he said. "You are a brave bird. Please, will you chase that billy goat out of the chili patch for me?"

The cock preened his feathers. "Why certainly,"
he said and strutted up to the goat.

"Billy goat! Billy goat! Get out of the chili
patch!" he crowed.

But the billy goat only waggled the other ear and
took another mouthful of leaves.

The cock ruffled his feathers. He stuck his
head forward and pecked sharply at the goat's
legs. "Go away! Go away!" he squawked.

The billy goat glared at the fighting cock.
"Go away yourself, you puffed-up bird! This is
my chili patch now!" And lowering his head,
the billy goat ran at the fighting cock and
tossed him out of the chili patch.

The cock picked himself up and shook his feathers into place. "I am sorry I cannot help you," he said to Pepito.

"Thank you for trying, Señor Cock," Pepito said.

Pepito sat down on a stone and put his chin
in his hands. "What am I going to do? If someone
doesn't chase the billy goat out of the chili patch
soon, the green leaves will all be gone," he said.

He looked down at the ground and saw a fire ant
carrying a grass seed. "Good-day, Señor Ant,"
Pepito said. "You are little, but you are wise.
Tell me, please, who can chase the billy goat
out of Mamacita's chili patch?"

"What will you give me if *I* chase him away?"
the fire ant asked.

"I will give you a whole bushel of corn,"
Pepito said.

The ant shook his head. "That is too much."

"I will give you a whole ear of corn."

"That is still too much."

"I will give you a few grains of corn, then."

"That will be fine," the fire ant said.

Pepito ran to his house and picked three
kernels from an ear of corn hanging near the
door. He brought them to the ant.

"You must grind them for me," the ant said.

Pepito ran down the hill again and ground the
three kernels into meal. He ran back to the ant
with the meal in his hand.

"Put the meal beside my house," the ant said.

Pepito put the meal near the anthill.

"Now I will chase the billy goat out of the chili patch for you," the fire ant said. He crawled up a chili stem. He crawled out onto a chili leaf.

Softly he dropped onto the billy goat's leg.
Up he crawled over the billy goat's hair. Up
and up he crawled until he reached the billy
goat's head. He crawled into the billy goat's
ear and gave him a fiery bite.

The billy goat danced about, shaking his head.
"Oh dear! Oh dear! What is biting my ear?" he
cried.

The fire ant only bit harder.

The billy goat kicked his heels in the air
and dashed out of the chili patch. The ant
dropped to the ground. The billy goat clattered
off down the hill.

"Thank you, Señor Ant, thank you!" Pepito exclaimed. "You have saved Mamacita's chili patch."

"It is nothing," the fire ant said and began to carry the cornmeal into his house.

Pepito ran down the hill and told his mother what had happened. "It is better to be little and wise, sometimes, than big and strong, is it not, Mamacita?" Pepito asked.

His mother smiled and gave Pepito a big hug. "Yes, my little one," she said.

The billy goat never came back. Pepito still
takes care of the chili patch. Every morning
he carries water up the hill for the chili plants.
Every evening he hoes the ground to keep the weeds away.

Pepito is proud of the chili patch.

Mamacita is proud of Pepito.

M
MAY